MW01033360
PET SIMULATOR™
TWO TALES OF
TEAMWORK

TWO TALES OF TEAMWORK

By Tracey West

Illustrations by
Vincent Batignole

SCHOLASTIC INC.

ISBN 978-1-5461-3159-5

10 9 8 7 6 5 4 3 2 1 25 26 27 28 29

Printed in the U.S.A. 37

First printing 2025

Book design by Martha Maynard

RIDDLE OF THE RAINBOW RAVINE

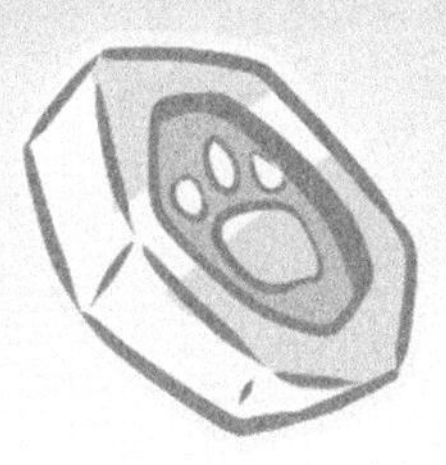

CHAPTER ONE

A small orange dog raced across the green grass. The corgi collided with a bale of hay.

"Kaboomie!" he yelled. The hay bale exploded and rained down on the grass.

A gray cat trotted up to him. "Ruffles,

what are you doing?" he asked. "We're supposed to be stacking these hay bales, not exploding them."

"Sorry, Whiskers," Ruffles said. "I can't help it. I love smashing into stuff. It's a beautiful day, and everybody else is out there demolishing stuff and scooping up coins and treasures."

Whiskers and Ruffles gazed past the farm where they lived. In the distance, they could see other pets racing down the pathways of their world or zipping along on hoverboards. The sounds of small explosions echoed through the world of Pet Simulator as pets smashed into

coin-filled presents, wooden crates, sparkly treasure chests, and more.

"We can go smash stuff after we clean up this mess. It won't take long," Whiskers promised.

"Okay," Ruffles replied. "I promise to get to work. First, I'll—hey, it's Penny!"

A blue unicorn trotted up to them. "Hey, Whiskers! Hey, Ruffles!"

Ruffles's tail wagged happily as he bounded toward Penny.

"Hi, Penny!" he cried, bouncing into the unicorn.

Penny laughed. "It's good to see you too, Ruffles. What are you and Whiskers doing at home on such a glittery, sparkly, perfectly beautiful day?"

"Just trying to clean up," Whiskers answered. "We're almost done. We'll be finished as soon as Ruffles stops exploding the hay bales."

"I can help you," Penny offered. "Then we can all go do something super-duper fun together."

"Sounds like a plan," Whiskers said. "We're stacking the hay bales over there."

Ruffles pushed one of the bales forward with his nose. "Got it! No kaboomies this time!"

But the hay bale wouldn't budge. He

grunted as he pushed forward. Then he stopped.

"There's something in the way." He peered around the bale. A big gray rock was blocking his path.

"This rock doesn't belong here," Ruffles said. "I know just what to do."

He reached into his backpack and took out a stick of TNT. "We just need a little extra help . . ."

"Ruffles, no!" Whiskers warned.

But Ruffles had already lit the TNT.

KABOOMIE! The rock exploded, showering them with gray dust. The hay bales closest to it also exploded, creating another big mess.

Penny's eyes grew wide. "That's one way to get rid of a big rock."

"Look at this mess!" Whiskers complained.

"Don't worry. I'll clean this up in no time." Ruffles pawed at the dirt, scooping up the rock dust. "Hey, what's this?"

Whiskers and Penny gathered around him. Where the rock had been was now a shallow hole. Inside the hole was a wooden box.

"It could be treasure!" Ruffles scooped it up and opened it. Then he frowned. "It's just an old piece of paper."

"Let me see that," Penny said. She unrolled the paper and gasped. "This looks like a treasure map! What a marvelously magical surprise!"

"No way!" Ruffles cried.

Whiskers peered at the map. "Let me see."

The map showed a route that led to what looked like a long, wide canyon.

"The Rainbow Ravine," Whiskers said. "I've never heard of this place."

Penny read out loud from the back of the map:

Follow the map to the Rainbow Ravine.

It holds a treasure like you've never seen.

Complete the challenges if you dare.

You'll receive powers beyond compare!

"Powers beyond compare," Ruffles whispered.

Whiskers's whiskers began to twitch. "Forget about cleaning up. Let's go on an adventure!"

CHAPTER TWO

"I've been saying all morning that we should get out and smash things!" Ruffles reminded his friends.

"We won't be *just* smashing things," Whiskers pointed out. "This is a real adventure! We've never gone much farther than the farm, Ruffles. This is our chance to explore. Who knows what we'll find?"

"Hopefully we'll find the treasure!" Penny added. "I know every zone inside and out, so I can be our guide. I also have some extra-special Speed potions I can share. We can use them for a boost, so we'll get there faster."

"Awesome!" Whiskers said. "Ruffles, we should pack our backpacks before we go. I think I've got some fruits that could be useful."

"I know just what to pack!" Ruffles cried, racing off. He returned a minute later with a bulging backpack.

"What's inside?" Penny asked.

Ruffles opened up the backpack to show them. The whole backpack was stuffed with TNT!

"Just in case we have to demolish anything," he said.

Whiskers shook his head. "Are you sure? After the accident you just caused?"

"Hey, we found the map, didn't we?" Ruffles pointed out.

Penny opened her backpack and took out three vials containing sparkly white liquid. She gave one to Whiskers and another to Ruffles.

"If we're ready to go, then let's gulp

down these Speed potions and get moving," Penny said.

The three friends guzzled their potions. Ruffles immediately started to run.

"Betcha can't catch me!" the dog cried.

Whiskers leaped after him, and Penny trotted. They quickly caught up.

"Ruffles, you don't have the map!" Whiskers reminded him.

"Oh yeah," Ruffles said, slowing down.

"I'll let my curly, swirly horn lead the way!" Penny cried, moving in front of him.

They swiftly moved through the zones, following the treasure map. They traveled through a valley of misty waterfalls where they saw a team of fireflies using TNT to blow up large safes. Coins clinked together as they exploded from the safes.

The map then led them into a spooky forest where bats smashed into moss-covered wooden crates.

They ran past giant mushrooms and forests of cotton-candy-colored trees. All around them, pets darted about, searching for coins, diamonds, and special treasures. But the three friends kept going.

Ruffles puffed and panted. "Are we there yet?"

"We're getting closer," Penny called back. "Just through these trees should be a cute little hill for us to climb."

They kept moving through the colorful trees until they reached the end of the forest. Rising in front of them was a tall, rocky mountainside.

"I thought you said it was a cute little hill?" Ruffles complained. "That mountain is monstrous!"

"Oh, it doesn't look so bad," Whiskers said. "Come on. We can do this!"

The Speed potions had worn off, so the friends made their way up the mountain slowly and steadily. As they got closer to the top, Whiskers's whiskers twitched.

"We're almost there. I can feel it!" he cried, his excitement rocketing him to the mountaintop.

"Penny! Ruffles! You need to see this!" he called back.

Penny and Ruffles caught up to him. Down below them stretched a deep ravine, a huge canyon between two mountain peaks. Each layer of the ravine sparkled with a different color of the rainbow. The brightly colored rock layers gleamed in the sunlight.

Penny gasped. "It's a shimmering, glimmering wonder of nature!"

Ruffles licked his snout. "Those layers remind me of a giant cake."

Whiskers charged ahead. "Let's go find the treasure!"

CHAPTER THREE

Whiskers, Ruffles, and Penny all scrambled down into the ravine. When they reached the rainbow layers, the rock under their feet became smooth and slick. They slid the rest of the way to the bottom.

"Whee!" cheered Whiskers.

"Wahoo!" cried Ruffles.

"How splendidly slippery!" Penny added.

They skidded to a stop in front of three giant, wooden crates. The first had a big

number "1" on the front. The second had a "2," and the third had a "3."

"These crates are blocking our way," Ruffles said. "Let's bust them!"

"Wait!" Whiskers cried, pointing. "There's a sign. Look."

Together they read:

open a single crate,
and pick the right one.
two will block your way,
while one leads to fun.
the right number is odd,
is what they say.
it's the number of pigs in a tale,
or meals in a day.

"An odd number would be one or three," Ruffles said.

"Right," Penny agreed. "And the answer must be three—like the story of the 'Three Little Pigs,' or three meals in a day."

"Three meals? I usually eat six," Ruffles replied.

"That's because you're always hungry, Ruffles," Whiskers said. "Anyway, there is no crate number six. Let's open crate number three!"

"On it!" Ruffles cried. He tossed some lit TNT at the third crate. "Kaboomie!"

The crate exploded! Colorful confetti danced in the air and a sheet of paper gently floated down. Penny grabbed it out of the air.

Congratulations! You may enter the ravine. You will have to complete five colorful challenges before you reach the treasure.

"Five challenges? No problem. We've got this," Whiskers said confidently.

"YES! Let's go!" Ruffles cheered.

The dog jumped up—and slammed into crate number two on the way back down.

BOOM! Crate 2 exploded.

The mountain rumbled, and suddenly rocks tumbled down the sides of the ravine.

"Everybody, run!!" Whiskers cried.

The three friends zoomed ahead and the rocks piled up behind them. Once at a safe distance, they stopped and turned back to look. The rockslide had blocked their path.

"Uh, sorry about that," Ruffles said. "That one was an accident."

Penny looked around nervously. "That was super-duper scary. It looks like these challenges could be dangerous."

Ruffles nodded. "Yeah. Are we sure about this?"

"I'm sure it will be okay," said Whiskers. "And besides, there's no other way to go but into the ravine. Come on, let's find that treasure!"

Whiskers ran ahead. Penny and Ruffles looked at each other and nodded. Then they sprinted after him.

Their dash through the ravine stopped at a red sign: the first challenge! Beyond it was a maze of red gift boxes, each one more than twice as tall as the pets.

Whiskers read from the sign.

THE RED CHALLENGE

get through the maze,
but don't get stuck in it!
after you enter,
the clock ticks down each minute.

The three friends looked up as a timer on a pedestal rose up in the center of the maze. It was set to three minutes.

"Three minutes! That's not a lot of time," Penny said with a frown. "Maybe we need some kind of plan."

"It's a maze! All we need to do is go through it fast. Follow me!" Whiskers instructed.

"Whiskers!" Penny called out, but as soon as the gray cat entered the maze, the timer started ticking. *2:59. 2:58.*

"Let's go," Ruffles said, and he and Penny chased after Whiskers.

The cat was running willy-nilly down each and every turn. When they caught up to him, he was stuck in a dead end.

"This maze is broken," Whiskers complained. "There's no way out of here."

Ruffles looked up at the clock. "Only two minutes left. We're wasting time."

"Let's try to retrace our steps," Penny

said. "We must have missed the path that leads out of here."

"Good idea!" Whiskers said, and he raced away again. Penny and Ruffles followed him to a fork in the maze. Whiskers skidded to a stop.

"Um, I think we go left," he said. "No, right. No, left!"

They all went left. Then right. Then left.

"Only thirty seconds to go!" Ruffles announced.

Another dead end!

"We're going to lose this challenge!" Whiskers wailed. "Maybe this was all a mistake."

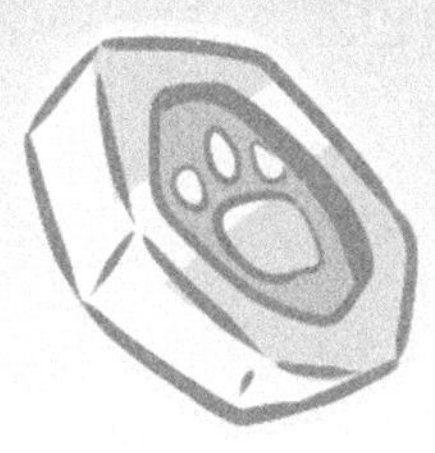

CHAPTER FOUR

"Maybe some unicorn magic can help," Penny suggested. She closed her eyes, and a trail of sparkly energy floated out of her horn.

She opened her eyes. "Hurry! Follow the sparkles!"

Penny trotted after the sparkly trail. Whiskers and Ruffles followed. They turned left, then right. Then left, then left again. Then right.

The clock ticked down to three . . .

two . . . one . . . just as the friends raced out of the maze!

"We did it!" Penny cried. "Super-duper job, everyone!"

Ruffles and Penny jumped up and down, but Whiskers hung back.

"I didn't do a super-duper job," Whiskers said sadly. "I was so excited to participate I almost lost us the challenge. I shouldn't have insisted on doing it my way from the beginning."

"That's okay," Penny told him. "Don't worry. We're going to ace our next challenge!"

"You think so?" asked Whiskers.

"Definitely, if we stick together," Ruffles said. "And I still think you're a great leader, Whiskers. Now take us to the next challenge!"

They ran to another sign. Whiskers read it out loud:

THE ORANGE AND YELLOW CHALLENGE

to get to the treasure,
you must cross the gap.
you have only three minutes,
so don't take a nap.
use coins and diamonds
to lower the bridge.

only then can you make your way to the next ridge.

They studied the challenge area. There was another clock, ready to tick down the time when they began. Past the sign was a field of wooden boxes. A row of orange trees bordered the left and right sides of the field.

The field ended at a huge gap in the ravine. A wooden drawbridge was perched on the edge. A large cauldron hung from a crank connected to the drawbridge.

Ruffles sniffed the air. "Those boxes are filled with coins and diamonds!"

"Right," Penny said. "Looks like we need to break the boxes and collect the coins and diamonds. Then we'll fill the cauldron with the loot to lower the drawbridge, to get to the other side of the ridge."

"That makes sense," Whiskers said. "But why is it called the Orange and Yellow Challenge?"

"I guess we'll find out," Penny said. "It's interesting, though, because orange and yellow are the next two colors in the rainbow after red. These challenges must be going in color order."

"We'll need lots of coins and diamonds to bring the bridge down," Ruffles said. "How about I blow up the crates—"

"And Penny and I can scoop up the coins and diamonds and fill the cauldron!" Whiskers finished.

Penny grinned. "Now that's totally terrific teamwork! Let's get this challenge started!"

"Kaboomie!" Ruffles yelled, and the first box exploded. The clock started ticking, and a small shower of yellow coins rained down, along with one diamond.

"We've got this!" Whiskers yelled, and he scooped up the coins. Penny picked up the diamond, and they carried them to the cauldron.

"Hey, these coins are yellow," Whiskers

remarked. "They must be the yellow part of the challenge."

"Good thinking, Whiskers," Penny said.

"Kaboomie!" Ruffles broke open the next box and Whiskers and Penny picked up the spoils. This time, no diamonds at all flew out.

"I wish these boxes had more

diamonds," Whiskers said as the coins clinked inside the cauldron. "We've been at this one whole minute, and the cauldron is barely full."

Penny glanced at the clock and frowned. "You're right, Whiskers. At the rate we're going, we'll never lower the bridge in time!"

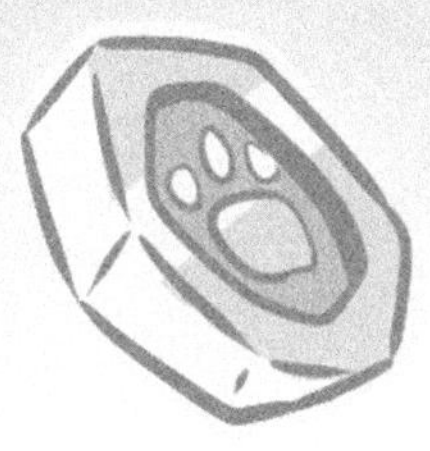

CHAPTER FIVE

Ruffles heard her. "I'm exploding things as fast as I can!"

"I know!" Penny called out. "We need to get more stuff out of those boxes. More diamonds would be nice. They're big and heavy."

Whiskers's nose twitched. "Wait. This is the Orange and Yellow Challenge, right? And there are oranges growing from those trees."

"And oranges boost diamond-collecting power!" Penny realized. "Quick, we all need to eat some."

Penny and Whiskers sped to the orange trees and each gobbled some fruits down. Then Whiskers tossed one to Ruffles.

"Ruffles, catch!"

The orange dog jumped up, caught an orange in his mouth, and landed back on the ground. Whiskers tossed him two more.

"Let's all demolish boxes now,"

Whiskers said. "And load that cauldron with diamonds!"

Ruffles smashed the next box. "Kaboomie!" This time, five diamonds flew out with the coins.

Smash! Bash! Whiskers and Penny crashed into the wood crates, and they splintered into pieces. Eight diamonds rained down, along with more yellow coins.

"Whoopee! Let's get these to the cauldron!" Penny cried.

The three friends worked together to smash the crates and fill the cauldron with the heavy diamonds. The clock continued to tick down.

Three . . . two . . .

"Last one!" Ruffles called out, tossing a diamond into the cauldron.

. . . *one!*

Full of coins and diamonds, the cauldron sank to the ground. The crank turned, and the drawbridge came down across the gap in the ravine.

"We did it!" Whiskers cheered, and he charged across the bridge, with Penny and Ruffles at his heels.

On the other side stood an enormous tree with a trunk as wide as the ravine. Large green leaves swayed on the tree's branches. A door was carved into the trunk, with a sign posted next to it.

THE GREEN CHALLENGE

answer the riddle to open the door:

i come in many colors but mainly green.

i'm often heard but not always seen.

bugs don't bug me like they do you.

i'm more likely found in a pond than a zoo.

i will not laugh if you tell me a joke.

it's far more likely that i will croak.

what am i?

The three friends studied the riddle.

"They're green and like bugs . . ." Whiskers muttered.

"And live in a pond . . ." Ruffles added.

"And croak," Penny finished. "They've got to be a frog!"

As she spoke, the door swung open.

RIBBIT!

A big, green frog jumped out! The frog knocked over Ruffles and hopped away.

"Hey, watch where you're hoppin'!" Ruffles complained, jumping back to his feet.

Whiskers had already run through the door. "You've got to see this!"

The next section of the ravine was a low carpet of mushrooms in all different colors. The sign in front only said one thing: THE BLUE AND INDIGO CHALLENGE. And, instead of a timer like the other challenges had, there was a large number four on a sign across the way.

"What's indigo?" Ruffles asked.

"Yeah, and what are we supposed to do, exactly?" Whiskers wondered.

"Indigo is a color that is blue mixed with purple. It's one of the colors in the rainbow," Penny answered. "And I think we have to hop on the mushrooms to get to the other side, but in a—"

"Let's go!" Ruffles cried. He jumped on the nearest mushroom, a yellow one.

Boing! The mushroom launched Ruffles high into the air.

Bam! He crashed back to the ground.

"Well, that didn't work," Ruffles said, shaking it off.

Across the field of mushrooms, the four changed to a three.

"Oh no!" said Whiskers. "Do we only

have four chances? Penny, I think we need a plan!"

"I'm guessing there is a pattern," said Penny.

"Maybe it's all blues!" said Ruffles. "Should I go?"

"Or it could be all indigos," said Whiskers.

"If it's the Blue *and* Indigo Challenge, maybe we need to try both," said Penny. "I think I figured it out!"

Penny jumped on the nearest blue mushroom, landing safely.

"So far so good. Keep going!" Whiskers cheered her on.

Penny jumped to the nearest indigo

mushroom, and the mushroom didn't push her off.

"Okay, I think the pattern is blue, indigo, blue, indigo," Penny told the others.

Whiskers jumped on the blue mushroom behind Penny. Then Penny moved to the next blue mushroom. Ruffles jumped on next, and the cat and corgi followed the unicorn across the mushroom maze.

When they all jumped off the last mushroom, they found themselves facing a giant violet safe.

"Violet is the last color in the rainbow!" Penny cried. "The treasure must be inside!"

CHAPTER SIX

THE VIOLET CHALLENGE

good for you,
you're almost there!
this safe does hold a treasure fair.

to enter the safe,
you won't need a key.
you must solve the code,
and here's a clue: three.
to solve the code,
you've only got three tries.
you must work together
to claim your prize!

"What code?" Ruffles asked, and they all leaned toward the safe.

On the safe door was a digital screen with a row of alphabet keys underneath:

A B C D E F G H I J K L M N O P Q R S T U V W X Y Z

And above the screen, in larger letters, was a row of nonsensical letters:

H X Y L L J F B

"This looks hard," Ruffles remarked. "Can't I just blow this up?"

"I don't know, Ruffles. You might destroy the treasure inside," Penny said. "Just like the hay bales this morning."

"The sign says we need to work together," Whiskers said. "We have three tries. Why don't we each come up with an idea?"

"That's not as much fun as blowing up the safe, but it does sound like a good plan," Ruffles admitted.

"There's a clue in the rhyme," Penny reminded them. "Three."

"Hmm," Whiskers said. "Maybe we have to type each of those letters in the weird word three times."

"That's a good guess," Penny agreed. "Why don't you try it?"

Whiskers typed in HHHXXXYYYLLLLLL JJJFFFBBB.

A red *X* flashed on the digital screen.

Whiskers frowned. "Rats!"

"That's okay, Whiskers. It was a good guess," Penny said. "I think you're onto something. Let me think . . . maybe it has something to do with the alphabet up above. The third letter of the alphabet is *C*. So what if we add *C* to the letters?"

"Give it a try," Whiskers urged.

Penny typed: CHCXCYCLCLCJCFCB.

Another red *X* flashed.

"Grimy gumdrops!" Penny cried. "We only have one more try. Sorry."

"That's okay, Penny. You did well," Whiskers said. "Ruffles, it's your turn."

Ruffles had a big grin on his snout. "I think I know it. It's kaboomie!"

Whiskers shook his head. "We already talked about that, Ruffles. Blowing up the safe won't work."

"No, I mean the word *kaboomie*," he said. "I got the idea when Penny pointed at the alphabet. If you jump three letters past each letter in the silly word, it spells *kaboomie*. It's a code. See?"

Ruffles pointed to the letters:

H = K

X = A

Y = B

L = O

L = O

J = M

F = I

B = E

"Ruffles, you are a super-duper smarty-pants!" Penny said.

"I couldn't have done this without the

two of you," Ruffles replied. "I'm gonna type it in."

He typed in: KABOOMIE.

A green check mark appeared on the screen! Whiskers grabbed the handle of the safe door and pulled it open.

A big, beautiful Rainbow Gem glittered inside. It gleamed with the rainbow's seven colors: red, orange, yellow, green, blue, indigo, and violet.

Whiskers took it out and held it up. The three friends stared at it for a moment in surprised silence.

"It's so beautiful," Penny whispered. She touched it with a hoof.

Ruffles put a paw on it. "It's glowing from within!"

The Rainbow Gem began to shine brighter and brighter. Rainbow light exploded from the gem and swirled around Whiskers, Ruffles, and Penny.

"Whoa! I feel powerful!" Whiskers exclaimed.

Penny's eyes were wide. "This is marvelously magical!"

Ruffles wagged his tail. "I feel like I could do anything!"

The rainbow light faded, and the gem vanished.

"That was awesome," Ruffles said.

Penny trotted in a circle. "Let's put this powerful feeling to good use and find another adventure!"

"I'm in!" Whiskers said. "As long as we do it together."

THE GREAT PET RACE

CHAPTER ONE

Powered up by the Rainbow Gem, Whiskers, Ruffles, and Penny zoomed through the zones. Sparkly rainbow light trailed in their wake. They jumped on boxes and crates and big metal safes.

Each one instantly burst open, no match for the powers of the Rainbow Gem.

"This is so much fun!" Ruffles cried.

Penny leaped into the air. "I can jump so high!"

"And I can run so fast!" Whiskers said, racing past them. Ruffles and Penny chased after him, toward the golden sands of the Beach zone, where they ran past the day care. Whiskers skidded to a stop, sending sand spraying everywhere.

"Achoo!" Ruffles sneezed. "Watch it, Whiskers!"

"Sorry, but I had to stop fast," Whiskers said. "Look!"

He pointed across the beach, where a

big banner on poles stretched across the sand announcing THE GREAT PET RACE. A bunch of pets were gathered at the starting line.

"A race is just the adventure we were looking for!" Whiskers said.

"How lucky we are to find it!" Penny said. "Let's go see what it's all about."

They made their way to the crowd, where a llama stood behind a long table. The sign on the table read:

ENTER THE GREAT PET RACE!

teams of three will sprint across the magical zones, facing fiercely

challenging obstacles along the way. the first team to reach the finish line will receive a lifetime supply of potions!

"That's an awesome prize," Ruffles said.

"And we are an awesome team!" Whiskers added. "I think we should enter."

"Let's do it!" Penny agreed.

They got in line to sign up for the race. At the front of the line were a Demolition Cat, a Lava Scorpion, and a Cyborg Bunny.

"Welcome to the Great Pet Race. What is your team name?" the llama in charge asked them, looking at her clipboard.

"We're Team Smash!" the Cyborg Bunny said. "'Cause we're gonna SMASH the competition!"

The Demolition Cat and Lava Scorpion high-fived. "Yeah!"

"Team name?" Whiskers repeated. Just ahead of them was a team made up of a monkey, a chicken, and a small brown dog shaped like a fluffy loaf of bread.

"That's a Bread Shiba," Penny whispered. "They are very rare!"

Whiskers tapped the monkey on the shoulder.

"Excuse me, but what's the deal with the team names?" he asked.

"Every team needs one," the monkey replied. "I wanted us to be called Team Bananas."

The Bread Shiba interrupted. "But we're Team Charmed! Because we've got luck on our side!"

"Cluck-cluck, luck is right!" added the chicken. "We are one lucky team."

"Thanks," Whiskers said. "And good luck in the race, Team Charmed!" He turned back to his friends. "All right, we need to come up with a team name, quick."

Ruffles wagged his tail. "I know. How about Team Kaboo—"

"NO!" said Whiskers and Penny.

"All right, you don't have to get all grumpy about it," Ruffles said.

"Sorry, Ruffles," Penny said. "It's just that our team is so much more than kaboomies. Our team is great because we're learning how to work together."

"Team Together?" Whiskers said. "The three of us, working in harmony."

"Ooh, how about Team Harmony? That has a nice ring to it," Penny suggested.

"I like it!" Ruffles agreed.

The llama at registration called out, "Next!"

Whiskers bounded up to the table. "We're Team Harmony, and we want to enter the Great Pet Race!"

THE GREAT PET RACE

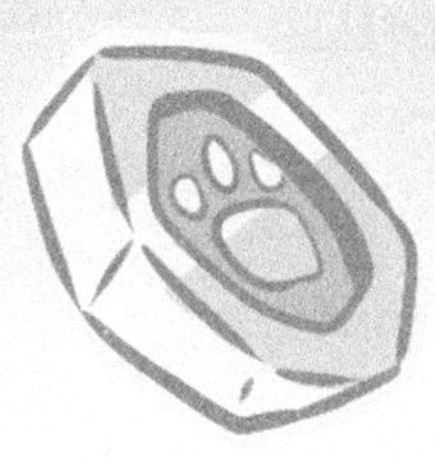

CHAPTER TWO

Tweeeeeeeeeeeeeeet!

A parrot flying overhead blew a whistle. "All teams report to the starting line!"

Team Harmony lined up with the others at the starting line painted in the sand, right where the beach met the ocean.

"I count ten teams in all," Ruffles reported.

"That's nice," Whiskers said, but he was more concerned about the location of the race than the teams. "Um, why are we so close to the water?"

Tweeeeeeeeet!

The parrot perched on a lifeguard chair. "Listen up, teams. The Great Pet Race will begin at the count of three. The first leg of the race is an ocean obstacle course. You need to jump across the floating platforms to reach the island in the distance. When you get there, jump on the hoverboards and move on to leg two. Got it? Good! Here we go. Three . . . two . . . *tweeeeeeet!*"

Everyone charged ahead—except for Whiskers. Ruffles noticed and hurried back to him. Penny followed.

"Whiskers, what's wrong?" Ruffles asked.

"I can't swim!" Whiskers said. "What if I fall in the water?"

"We won't let you fall," Penny promised. "We're a team, remember?"

Whiskers nodded. "That's right. And I'm not going to hold us back. I will overcome my fears. Let's go!"

The other teams had a head start, but Team Harmony quickly caught up, still powered by the Rainbow Gem.

Meanwhile, the other teams had already begun jumping from platform to platform. While the platforms were anchored down, they still wobbled and swayed whenever a pet landed on them.

Splash!

The chicken from Team Charmed had fallen in and was flapping her wings in the water.

Whiskers took a step back. "I don't know about this. She can fly, and even she couldn't stay out of the water! I'm just a cat!"

"Stay between me and Ruffles," Penny said, moving to Whiskers's side. "You're not a good swimmer, but you're a great jumper! We'll all jump together. Three, two, one, jump!"

They all jumped and landed on the nearest platform. It wobbled under their feet. Whiskers let out a big breath of relief.

Ruffles bounded to the platform's edge. "Look! The water's so clear! I can see a crab, and a blue fish, and a pink fish . . ."

"Focus, Ruffles," Whiskers said. "You're rocking the platform."

"And we've got to catch up to the other teams," said Penny.

Team Smash was way ahead of everybody, jumping from platform to platform with great force. Each time they landed, waves splashed the other teams, and all the platforms wobbled.

"Yeah! We are SMASHING this challenge!" yelled the Cyborg Bunny.

Ahead of Team Harmony, Team Charmed was still having trouble. The monkey and Bread Shiba were great jumpers, but the chicken was not. Each time she jumped off the platform, she took a short hop right into the water and the others stopped to help her climb up.

"Cluck-cluck!"

Team Harmony jumped past them. Sticking together, they jumped from platform to platform. They even caught up to Team Smash!

"I can see the island now," Whiskers told his team. "Only a few jumps left!"

On the platform up ahead, the Demolition Cat, Lava Scorpion, and Cyborg Bunny took a mighty leap.

"MEGA-JUMP!" yelled the Cyborg Bunny, and they landed on the next platform with their biggest, most massive jump yet.

WHOMP! A huge wave splashed up and knocked down Whiskers, Penny, and Ruffles. The platform they were standing on tipped sideways, and all of them tumbled into the ocean. The waves carried the three friends in three different directions.

"Help!" Whiskers yelled. "I can't swim!"

CHAPTER THREE

Whiskers felt two wet, furry arms around his waist. It was the monkey from Team Charmed!

"I've got you," he said, and he pulled Whiskers up onto the final platform.

Whiskers shook the water from his fur.

"Thanks. That was really nice of you," he said.

Penny and Ruffles climbed up onto the platform.

"Whiskers! I'm so sorry! That wave came out of nowhere!" Penny cried.

"It's okay, I got help from—" Whiskers looked at the monkey. "Er, what's your name?"

"Milo," the monkey replied. "And that's Coco the Chicken and Yumi the Bread Shiba. I'd better catch up to them!"

"Sure, and thanks again!" Whiskers called out as Milo leaped to the next platform.

"What a nice dude," Ruffles remarked.

"He stopped to help you in the middle of a race."

"Yes, Team Charmed really is charming!" Penny said with a giggle. "Whiskers, can we jump to the last platform together? Team Smash is already on the island, so there shouldn't be any more surprises."

"Sure," Whiskers replied. "One . . . two . . . three!"

The three friends jumped to the last platform, and then to the island, where hoverboards were waiting for all the contestants. Most of the teams had already zipped away.

The parrot flew in front of them.

"Hurry! Hurry! On to the next leg of the challenge!" he squawked.

"Hoverboards! That's more like it," Whiskers said, jumping onto a smooth hoverboard.

Penny and Ruffles each jumped on one.

"Let's follow the other racers, Team Harmony!" Whiskers called out.

They zoomed across the island to Shanty Town, where they found the other teams smashing into wooden crates.

The parrot squawked instructions. "Smash the crates! Find a shovel! Then head east to the desert!"

They jumped off their hoverboards. Team Smash was already holding up a Platinum Shovel in victory.

"Once again, we SMASHED this challenge!" cried the Cyborg Bunny. "This Platinum Shovel has awesome digging power."

Bam! Coco the Chicken smashed into a crate. A Gold Shovel flew out and Milo the Monkey jumped up and caught it. "Wowee! A Gold Shovel! We can dig awesomely fast with this."

Yumi the Bread Shiba jumped up and down. "That's the best shovel! We sure got lucky!"

"Come on, Team Harmony, let's start smashing!" Whiskers urged.

Ruffles headbutted a wooden crate. He shattered it into pieces, but there was no shovel inside.

Wham! Penny smashed open another wooden crate, but there was no shovel in there, either.

Bam! Whiskers body-slammed a wooden crate, turning it into a pile of splinters. "Rats! No shovel!" he wailed. He looked at Penny. "Can unicorn magic help us now?"

"Maybe," Penny said. "Let me try."

A light shone from Penny's horn. She aimed it at a crate, and the pets could see what was inside! This one was empty.

"Try again," Whiskers urged.

Penny aimed at another crate, and another. Then she shone a light on a crate, and they saw the shape of a shovel inside.

"I've got this!" Ruffles cried.

SLAM! He demolished the crate, and a wooden shovel flew out. He grabbed it.

"It's a Flimsy Shovel, the slowest shovel there is," Penny said. "Should we try to find a better one?"

"We're too far behind," Whiskers said. "I say we hurry to the next zone."

"Sounds like a plan!" Ruffles said. "If we move fast, maybe we can make up for the digging speed!"

Penny nodded. "I agree!"

Team Harmony raced toward the next leg of the challenge.

CHAPTER FOUR

Whiskers, Ruffles, and Penny caught up to the other teams in the Great Pet Race. They stopped in the Desert Pyramids: a large, wide stretch of sand.

The parrot squawked into a megaphone so everyone could hear: "There are ten Charm Stones buried somewhere in this desert. Dig until you find one, and then move to the puzzle pen to find a cannon that will get you to the next zone."

He pointed to a fenced-in area on the edge of the desert.

The three friends gazed at the desert. Each team had only one shovel, and everyone with a shovel was busy digging in the sand while their teammates cheered them on.

"Ugh, what's the point?" Whiskers asked with a sigh. "My fur is wet. Everyone has a better shovel than we do. We'll never catch up!"

Ruffles started digging with the Flimsy Shovel. "Don't worry, Whiskers. I'm a fast digger, and I've still got some of that Rainbow Gem power. We'll catch up."

His tail wagged as he dug with the flimsy shovel. His arms moved so fast they were a blur!

Then he stopped. "Nothing here. Let's find another spot." He started to run off.

"Wait, Ruffles!" Penny called out. "I think I have a plan."

Ruffles trotted back.

"See how everyone is just digging in random spots?" she asked. "Well, I think we can make a simple grid of this area here, and you can dig one square in the grid at a time. That will increase our odds of finding a Charm Stone."

"Great plan!" Ruffles cheered.

Penny used her hooves to start drawing the grid in the sand.

"Whiskers, can you help me draw the grid?" Penny said.

"You don't need my help," Whiskers said grumpily. "Let me just bask here in the sun and dry off."

Penny frowned but didn't push Whiskers. She drew a row of squares, and Ruffles resumed his speedy digging.

"Go, Ruffles, go!" Penny cheered as she moved to draw the next row of the grid.

Across the desert, Milo's voice rose up. "Lucky us! Team Charmed found the first Charm Stone!" He held up a clump of multicolored, sparkly crystals.

Whiskers said, "See what I mean?"

"Come on, Whiskers, there are plenty of other teams still digging. Even Team

Smash hasn't found a stone yet," Ruffles pointed out as he dug in another square.

Nearby, the Cyborg Bunny was frustrated. "Argh! I want to SMASH this shovel!"

"Okay, Ruffles, move on to the next row," Penny instructed.

"Got it!" Ruffles replied. He jumped to the next square and started to dig again. Sand flew everywhere. Then he let out a cry.

"Look! A Charm Stone!"

A clump of multicolored crystals sparkled in his paw.

Penny ran over to him. Whiskers perked up and joined them.

"You did a super-duper spectacular job, Ruffles!" Penny said.

"No way! I can't believe you found it so fast!" said Whiskers.

"That's what good teamwork and a plan can do," said Penny.

"Go Team Harmony!" said Ruffles.

Whiskers looked at his paws. "I'm sorry I gave up. We're a team, and I let you down."

"It's okay, Whiskers. Everyone needs a break sometimes. Come on, let's get to the puzzle pen! I know you can get there faster than any of us." Ruffles took off running, and Whiskers and Penny chased after him.

They reached the puzzle pen. The parrot was perched on one corner of the fenced-in area holding a row of cannons. Team Charmed was already inside.

"How do we get in?" Ruffles asked.

"Look! Each entry gate has a puzzle board on it," Penny said. "I think we need to move the pieces around until the puzzle is complete. Then the door will open."

"Right! Solve the puzzle! Solve the puzzle!" squawked the parrot.

"What's our plan, Penny?" Whiskers asked.

Penny stared at the puzzle board. The puzzle pieces were magnetically attached to the board, in bright colors of green, yellow, blue, and pink.

"Hmm," Penny said. "This looks like just a bunch of colors."

Whiskers looked at the Charm Stone in Ruffles's paw. "Wait," he said. "Those are the same colors as the Charm Stone. Maybe that's what the puzzle solution is! A picture of a Charm Stone!"

"I think you're onto something, Whiskers," Penny said, and she quickly moved the puzzle pieces around. "Green on the left . . . two blue crystals in the middle . . . pink crystal on the right . . ."

"Yellow goes above the pink," Whiskers coached.

"And there's a blue crystal on the bottom right too," Ruffles added.

Penny slid the last piece into place.

"Finished!" she cried, and the gate swung open. "That was great teamwork, everyone."

The three of them dashed into the pen.

"Use the cannons to get to the next challenge!" the parrot instructed.

Whiskers, Ruffles, and Penny each climbed into a cannon.

Boom! Boom! Boom!

The three pets soared through the air to the next challenge.

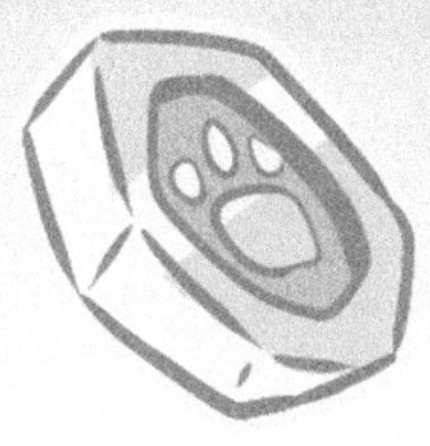

CHAPTER FIVE

Whiskers, Ruffles, and Penny landed in the base of the Mountains, where another parrot was waiting for them. There were no other teams in sight.

"Looks like everyone else has a head start," Ruffles remarked.

"We are not giving up yet," Whiskers said, his voice now determined. "We're still in this."

The parrot gave instructions. "In this leg of the challenge, you need to jump from ledge to ledge until you reach the top of that mountain." The parrot pointed to the tall peak with a wing.

"But first, crack open that Charm Stone! It might hold a charm that will help you in this challenge," the parrot added.

Whiskers and Penny turned to Ruffles.

"You know what to do," Whiskers told him.

Ruffles grinned. "Kaboomie!"

Ruffles smashed open the Charm Stone. A sparkly, light-blue gem shaped like a diamond tumbled out.

"A Diamond Charm!" Penny cried. "That would be great if we were harvesting diamonds, but it won't help us get up the mountain."

"Then we'll just have to do our best," Whiskers said. "Let's go, Team Harmony!"

They all jumped together onto the first rocky ledge jutting out of the mountain. They gazed up. To get to the top, they'd have to jump from ledge to ledge. On the next ledge, they saw a glint of green.

"That's Team Charmed," Penny said. "And it looks like they've got an Agility Stone."

"No fair," Whiskers grumbled. "They got lucky again!"

"They're called Team Charmed, remember?" Penny asked.

Ruffles laughed. "Maybe next time, we should call ourselves Team Nobody Can Beat!"

"Let's become Team on the Move and start this climb," Whiskers urged.

They all jumped to the second ledge.

"I like this course," Whiskers remarked. "There's no water. The platforms aren't moving. It's like one giant cat scratching post!"

Ruffles's ears drooped. "It's really high up there."

"Just don't look down, Ruffles, and you'll be fine," Penny said. "We'll make each jump together so you won't be alone."

"That's been a great strategy for Team Harmony so far," said Whiskers. "The team that jumps together stays together!"

They jumped to the next ledge and caught up to Team Charmed.

Milo the Monkey, Coco the Chicken, and Yumi the Bread Shiba quickly bounced to the next ledge with ease.

"This Agility Charm is awesome!" Milo cried.

"Come on, team," Whiskers said. "We don't need an Agility Charm to win this. Let's go!"

CHAPTER SIX

"Three, two, one, jump!"

Whiskers, Ruffles, and Penny leaped to the next ledge, at the heels of Team Charmed.

They jumped from one ledge to another, higher and higher, until . . .

"We are SMASHING this challenge!"

They jumped to the very top of the mountain. They had caught up to Team Smash!

The Cyborg Bunny turned and glared at Team Harmony with his glowing blue eye.

"Do you really think you can beat us?" he taunted. "Nobody can beat Team Smash!"

"Oh yeah? Well, don't count out Team Harmony. We never give up!" Whiskers said.

Penny tugged on Whiskers's arm. "Ignore them, Whiskers. We've got a race to win!"

They ran across the snow.

"We're near Ski Town," Penny remarked. "These are the Icy Peaks."

Ten colorful flags poked out of a mount of snow. Each flag had a different boosting effect.

A parrot flew overhead. "Choose a flag to help you with the final challenge! The flag's boost will help your team."

"What *is* the final challenge?" Penny asked.

"Can't tell you. *Squawk!*" the parrot replied.

They stared at the flags. "Hmm," Penny said. "We should choose carefully."

Just then, Milo sped past them and grabbed an orange flag with paw prints on it. "Woo-hoo! This Hasty Flag will boost our speed!" Then he hurried back to his team.

"Rats!" Whiskers cried. "That was a good one."

He glanced behind him. Team Smash was charging toward the flags.

"Quick! We need to choose!" he cried.

Ruffles grabbed a purple flag with a muscled arm symbol on it. "Let's take the Strength Flag! That might come in handy."

"Good choice, Ruffles!" Penny agreed. "Let's go!"

They ran across the snow toward a banner reading: FINAL CHALLENGE OF THE GREAT PET RACE. They gazed down into an icy crevasse. Jagged chunks of ice stuck out on the path. In the distance, they saw a large red flag with the words: FINISH LINE.

"I guess the Strength Flag won't help us jump over these icy obstacles," Ruffles remarked. "Sorry."

"That's okay!" Whiskers said. "Let's get

moving! Team Charmed is already way ahead of us."

They jumped into the crevasse and zipped along the slippery course, jumping over the ice obstacles. About halfway through, they heard a scream.

"Cluck-cluck, HEEEEEEEEEELP!"

Team Charmed was in trouble!

Yumi the Bread Shiba was clinging to the edge of the ice track with one paw. With his other paw, he held the hand of Milo, who dangled beneath him. And Milo held on to Coco's wing.

"Help us!" Yumi cried. "Our Hasty Flag made us go too fast on the ice, and we slipped!"

Whiskers looked at his teammates. "We've got to help them."

"But we'll lose our lead," Ruffles said.

"Milo helped me before," Whiskers reminded him. "It's the right thing to do."

Ruffles planted the Strength Flag in the ice. "Looks like this extra strength boost is going to come in handy after all."

Ruffles grabbed on to Yumi. Penny and Whiskers wrapped their arms around Ruffles.

"One . . . two . . . three . . . PULL!" Ruffles cried.

Boosted by the power of the Strength Flag, and with a mighty heave, they hoisted Yumi, Milo, and Coco back onto the icy track.

"Thank you so much!" Milo said.

"No problem," Whiskers replied. "Now we just gotta—"

The Cyborg Bunny, Lava Scorpion, and Demolition Cat sped by.

"You've just been PASSED by Team SMASH!" yelled the Cyborg Bunny.

"We're too shaken up to keep going," Milo said. "Go get them, Team Harmony! You can do it."

Whiskers, Ruffles, and Penny hurried to catch up with Team Smash. They jumped over obstacle after obstacle, keeping their footing on the slippery ice. But they couldn't catch up.

"Look, Team Smash is almost at the finish line!" Ruffles called out.

"We're gonna SMASH the Great Pet Race!" Cyborg Bunny cried. "Let's SMASH this last jump!"

All at the same time, Team Smash hurled themselves over the last obstacle.

BAM! They landed with great force.

The ice underneath them cracked!

Team Harmony skidded to a stop. They watched as Team Smash fell through the ice, onto the level below.

Penny gazed down. The pets groaned on the ice, but they were moving. "They're okay!"

Whiskers tugged at her. "Then let's go! We can finish this thing."

The three friends looked at the broken ice. "Let's jump together?" asked Ruffles. Penny and Whiskers nodded. Together, Team Harmony jumped over the broken ice. They streaked past the finish line flag. A crowd of pets clapped and cheered for

FINISH

them. And a flock of parrots flew overhead.

"*Squawk!* The winner of the Great Pet Race is Team Harmony!"

Whiskers, Ruffles, and Penny jumped up and down and hugged one another.

"This is the most super-sparkly feeling ever!" Penny cried.

"I can't believe we won!" added Ruffles.

"Yes, and we did it as a team," Whiskers said. He grinned. "I guess Team Harmony was the best name for us after all."

A parrot flew over to them with a pouch. "Congratulations on winning your lifetime supply of potions. We'll start you with just a sample."

They looked inside the bag. "Wow!" said Ruffles. "Damage potions! Just think of all the kaboomies!"

"And Lucky Egg potions!" said Penny. "It's not just Team Charmed that has the luck now!"

"And most importantly, Treasure Hunter potions!" said Whiskers. "Which we'll need for all the future adventures we're going to go on together."

"Just as long as we can take a nap first," said Ruffles. "It's been a big day."

"Good thing we cleaned up *before* we left, right?" said Whiskers.

"Didn't you leave a big hole in the ground?" asked Penny.

Ruffles yawned. "That's tomorrow's problem. I'm sure filling the hole will be its own adventure."

"It will be if you insist on using more TNT," said Whiskers. "Come on, let's go home."

ABOUT THE AUTHOR

Tracey West is the author of the *New York Times* bestselling series Dragon Masters, for Scholastic Branches. She has written more than 400 books for children, including the Underdogs series, illustrated by Kyla May; the Pixie Tricks series, illustrated by Xavier Bonet; and the perennially popular Pokémon chapter books. She lives with her husband, adopted dogs, and chickens in the western Catskill mountains of New York State.

ABOUT THE ILLUSTRATOR

Born in the southwest of France, Vincent was raised with lots of French comics, colorful anime on TV, and his grandparents' collection of true crime books. This is surely how he developed his taste for creating cute, absurd, and creepy stories. Trained at the École Pivaut in Nantes, his professional journey started in 2005 with the comic series GloomCookie, created by Serena Valentino (Disney's Villains book series) and Ted Naifeh (Courtney

Crumrin series). Since then, he's been illustrating and writing for various international clients while earning a master's degree in cinema history and film analysis.

Vincent now lives in Paris with his dog, Kero, surrounded by what's easily one of the biggest collections of manga drawn by CLAMP.